HOW TO BE COOLER THAN COOL

For Ada, one cool chick
S.T.

For Lou and Hugo, the coolest Wolf and Bear around
J.J.

First published 2021 by Walker Books Ltd, 87 Vauxhall Walk, London SE11 5HJ • This book has been typeset in URW Egyptienne T and Futur[a] Bold • Printed in China • British Library Cataloguing in Publication Data: a catalogue recor[d] for this book is available from the British Library • ISBN 978-1-4063-7826-9 • www.walker.co.uk • 10 9 8 7 6 5 4 3 2

Sean Taylor Jean Jullien

HOW TO BE COOLER THAN COOL

Look what Cat found.

These sunglasses.

COOL.

"You know what," she said.

"I'm not just any old cat at the playground.
I'm a real cool cat who can glide backwards down the slide, looking cooler than cool ...
WITH EXTRA COOL ON TOP!"

YEAH!

But...

UH OH!

MEOOOAAAAWWW!

Now look what Cockatoo has found...

GROOVY.

"You know what," he said.
"I'm not just any old cockatoo.
I'm a supercool cockatoo
who can dance coolly along the see-saw,
doing the supercool cockatoo boogaloo!"

I'M TOO COOL FOR SCHOOL!

But...

UH OH!

OH NO!

AAAWK!

And guess what Pig found...

HEY, MAN.

"You know what," he said.
"I'm not just any old pig.
I'm a totally cool pig who can
stand up on the swing looking
so completely cooler than cool
that everyone's going to call me
Mr Totally Completely Cool!"

Pig smiled.

"EVEN
MY
PANTS
ARE
COOL."

YEAH, BABY!

But...

UH OH!

OH NO!

WOAH!

OINK!?

Pig said, “I don’t think I managed to look cooler than cool just then.”

Cat and Cockatoo shook their heads. “You didn’t.”

Then Cat said,
"You don't look cool when
you've got sunglasses
on your bottom."

They were all disappointed.

The sunglasses didn't make them cool, after all.

MMM...
NOT EXACTLY COOL AS CHRISTMAS...
SHEESH!

Then Chick came along.

“Oh YEAH!” she said. “Look what I’ve found!”

“Watch out!” Cockatoo told her.

Cat added, “They’ll make you try to
glide coolly down the slide,
or dance coolly along the see-saw,
or stand up coolly on the swing.”

“BUT IT WON’T BE COOL!” said Pig.

Chick still put them on.

She said, "I'm just going to slide down the slide,
see-saw on the see-saw,
and swing on the swing.

Come on!"

They did. Nobody tried to be cool.

Soon they were sliding,

see-sawing and swinging together.

And you know what ...

that was cooler than cool.